LU WAR

STORMY MEYER

STORMY MEYER

outskirts
press

Outskirts Press, Inc.
http://www.outskirtspress.com

ISBN: 978-1-9772-0385-4

Cover Photo © 2019 gettyimages.com. All rights reserved - used with permission. Interior Images by Stormy Meyer

Outskirts Press and the "OP" logo are trademarks belonging to Outskirts Press, Inc.

PRINTED IN THE UNITED STATES OF AMERICA

To Vivi
For always being there for me,
Enjoying my work,
And overall being an amazing friend.
And to Mrs. Shultz
For being an amazing teacher

NOTE FROM LUCAS

Hello! I'm Lucas, as you can see. I am writing down these events in hope that it might help you if you ever end up in a crazy situation like I did. Now before you begin reading, I want to explain a few things, because if I don't, this story will be very confusing.

First of all, you should get to know the gods. There are three: Kalos, Katastrofi, and Issrropia. They usually act like normal people but they are absolutely not.

They all have basic powers to go along with their own, such as being able to "jump" through time and space, mind reading, cool stuff like that to put it simply!

Kalos is the god of basically everything good. He has two followers: the two lovers, Jake and Noelle.

Katastrofi is quite the opposite. He is the god of evil and death. Max is his only follower, but he is extremely powerful.

And last but most definitely not least: Issrropia. She is the goddess of balance. If you haven't guessed already, she is the one I follow. She only chooses sides if she must; she's neutral.

Second thing you should know: this world is full of magic. It takes a lot of energy, but if someone is desperate it might come easily. There are a lot of things you can do with it.

If someone was in battle and had no weapon, they could pretty much create one out of thin air. This works very well, but the weapon usually breaks when it has no more purpose.

You can also use magic to heal. If someone is wounded, there are quite a few ways you can heal them with magic. The most common is chanting.

The last option is downright evil. It can be used to destroy almost anything, from a small house to entire nations. Though this side of magic is strictly forbidden, some still practice it in secret...

The last thing I wanted to tell you is that this land is not very big, as far as we have explored. But just in case, I will add a few maps, notes, and pictures that might help your journey.

I hope this information helps you understand this story better and that it might lead you on your way. I also hope that when you do find your way here, the wars are over, and peace rules the land. If not, save my homeland for me.

In hope and helpfulness,
Lucas

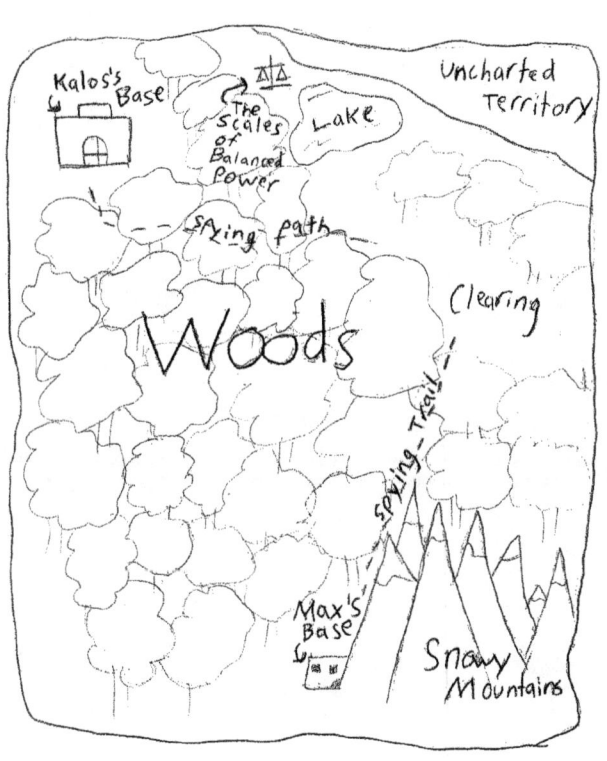

1

SPYING

I stood outside Max's door, silently listening to him go over his plans, unaware of me spying on him. Being a follower of Issrropia, I hated the idea of choosing sides, but because of the damage that he had done to the Scales of Balanced Power, I had no choice but to create an alliance with Kalos, and this is what Jake and Noelle needed to be done.

When I heard Max walking towards the door, I booked it. I ran quietly through the halls, following and adding to the mental map in my head. I glanced over my shoulder, just for a second, to make sure he wasn't following me. SMACK! The next thing I know I'm on the ground, Max holding me down with a glare on his face.

"Well, well, well. An Issrropia follower, spying? Katastrofi is going to find this very interesting." He stood, then forced me to stand up too.

"Walk." He led me through a maze of halls. We

stopped walking after a few minutes, and he shoved me through the door. I looked around and realized it was his jail. He pushed me into one of the cells and locked the door.

"I think I'll let Katastrofi take care of you," he said and walked away, leaving me to my thoughts. I paced back and forth through my cell, taking in my surroundings.

The jail was somewhat dark, the only light coming from a few torches placed on the walls. Waterdrops occasionally dripped from the ceiling and ran down the walls.

Everything in the small, damp jail was made from stone and iron bars. I should have brought my pick axe; then I would have been home free. But I had left all my important stuff in my base, including my magic bow and armor from Issrropia, my enchanted sword, and my journal from Kalos. All I had was food, which I guess was good. Then if Max searched me he wouldn't find anything important. But if he found my base...that would be more than bad.

The Scales
of
Balanced Power

- Represents Issrropia
- Shows who has more power
- Usually balanced
- One side Good, one side Evil

2

EVIL'S RETURN

I was snapped out of my thoughts when the door slammed open. Max was standing in the doorway, a smile on his face. His eyes looked tired yet excited, the way they always did after he prayed to Katastrofi. I knew from experience that successfully praying for a god to do something took a lot of energy. Max grabbed my shoulder and pulled me to my feet.

"Lord Katastrofi has arrived," he said with a hint of excitement.

I didn't move. I sighed and crossed my arms, a small smirk appearing on my face when I decided what I was about to say.

"I may be in your base, Max, but that does not make Katastrofi my lord. I still worship Lady Issrropia." I smiled as he turned red. It had always been my typical slightly know-it-all attitude that got him upset.

"Just get over here." That was all he said. He dragged me out of the cell and down one hall, then stopped. He tied something around my head, obscuring my vision. Then he led me the rest of the way. When he took the blindfold off, we were standing in front of an iron door. He took a key out of his pocket and unlocked it.

When I stepped in I was shocked to see that I was standing in a temple. It was made of blood-colored bricks and dark wood. In the center was a black altar, but it was what was in front of it that made my blood run cold.

There was a man with his back turned to us. His skin was blood red and his midnight-black hair almost covered his devilish horns. When he turned his smirk made my eyes grow wide in fear. Katastrofi had returned.

Katastrofi

God of Evil

- Name means distruction
- Firey staff
- Has devil horns
- Represented by obsidian, ruby, and fire
- Has 1 follower

3

CHOICES

Max shoved me forward to stand before Katastrofi. He forced me to my knees, then bowed to his lord. Katastrofi nodded at him as if dismissing him. Max smiled and stepped to the side. Katastrofi then turned to me.

"Lucas..."

I glared up at him, though I was unable to move because Max had tied my hands behind my back. My day had gone from great, to good, to okay, to bad, to downright awful. Meeting the god of all things evil was not on my list of things to do today. Actually, it wasn't on the list of things to do ever.

"Issrropia choosing sides, eh? Well, this can only mean one thing: war. You, Lucas, have made a mistake, siding with Kalos. But I'll give you a choice." He paused, probably smiling, but my eyes were locked on the floor. This was bad.

"You can join me, be my spy...or you can choose the other option: death."

My heart skipped a beat. I had expected worse, but being Katastrofi's spy? That would be betraying Issrropia. I locked eyes with him and glared. "Never." He sighed and shook his head. *Please, Issrropia, please. I need a little help, just this once.*

"Fine then." A pitch-black sword appeared in his hand. I lowered my head again, my eyes squeezed shut, my lips moving in a silent prayer. *Please, Issrropia, please.*

A vision flashed through my mind. A young woman wearing a golden dress with dark blue outlines was crouching next to me, her hand on my knee, her golden chain wristband almost touching me. Her golden hair flowed over her shoulders, the blue tips shining. Her navy-blue eyes looked deeply into mine from under her gold circlet crown, which was decorated with blue sapphires. Lying on the ground next to her was a gold staff with blue gems on it, and a small engraving of a balance scale. *The Scales of Balanced Power...* She was smiling, and I smiled back.

"Issrropia!" She nodded excitedly and hugged me. I almost fainted, being hugged by a goddess.

"Lucas! It is very nice to see you again. Too bad it has to be at such a rough time. But I am here to help." I nodded, showing I was listening. She took a deep breath.

"Okay. As soon as you open your eyes, you will

know what to say. Oh, and Lucas, can you promise me something?" I nodded again. "No matter what happens, you must trust me, got it?"

I smiled and bowed my head. "Yes, my lady."

She put on a sweet smile, then waved and disappeared. Before I opened my eyes, I felt the ropes binding my hands harden, then shatter. I opened my eyes to see Katastrofi's sword coming down on me, though it seemed to be in slow motion.

"I trust you, Issrropia," I whispered. Then, in a surge of confidence, I jumped up and knocked the sword out of his hand. I turned to Max, who was standing by the wall, watching in shock.

I glanced down to discover that my armor had appeared on my body, my bow in my hand. My enchanted sword was strapped to my waist. The light blue magic glow from my gear was bright and alive.

I lunged at Max and tackled him to the ground, putting my sword to his neck. His eyes were wide, but then he smiled and stopped trying to break free. Suddenly, a strong hand grabbed my neck and pulled me off Max.

Issrropia
God of Balance

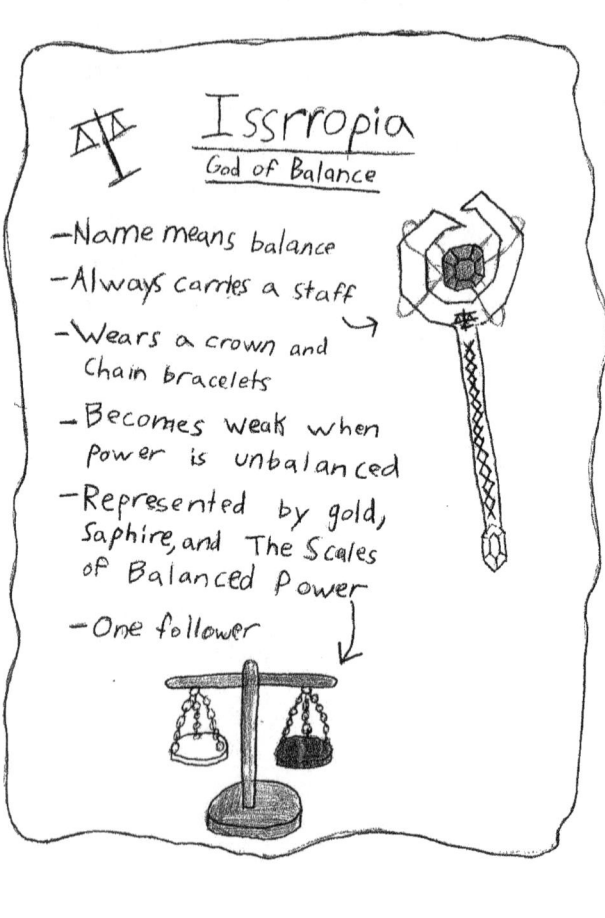

- Name means balance
- Always carries a staff →
- Wears a crown and chain bracelets
- Becomes weak when power is unbalanced
- Represented by gold, Saphire, and The Scales of Balanced Power
- One follower

4

DEALS

"Drop the weapons, Lucas, or else." I dropped the weapons, but I didn't stop struggling against his iron grip. Katastrofi tightened his grip on my neck, choking me and making it impossible to breathe. *I trust you, Issrropia.*

When my struggling slowed due to loss of air, he dropped me onto the floor. As I lay on the ground, staring at the ceiling, trying to catch my breath, I thought I saw a flash of gold and blue. *Issrropia? But that's not possible.*

After a few more minutes of trying to catch my breath, I sat up onto my knees. I took another shaky breath and looked up at Max and Katastrofi. Both of them had their arms crossed and a scowl on their face.

"Are we done playing games?" asked Katastrofi.

I couldn't answer. All I could do was stare at the

floor, taking deep breaths, but I slowly started nodding my head. Yes, I was done. Yes, I had given up. Yes. Yes. Yes.

Katastrofi smiled and knelt next to me. "Good. Now here is what is going to happen…" He explained that I was going to be a spy for him, tell him about what Kalos was planning. I felt bad about lying to Jake and Noelle, and lying to a god was deadly, and I would be lying to two, one of whom I worshiped. But it not only meant saving my life—it was my only chance to do my job: keep the peace. This was my last chance to stop a war… I had no choice anyway.

Katastrofi turned to Max and spoke to him, no doubt giving orders, but I was too fazed to listen. Spying? Max walked over and pulled me to my feet. He led me through the halls, so many I couldn't possibly remember all of them. When we got to the entrance to the base, he stopped and turned to me.

"You are to report to me whenever possible. Oh, and if you think you can get away without coming back, you are most definitely wrong. Now go." He pushed me through the door and locked it shut behind me. With that I started walking towards Kalos' base.

5

KALOS' BASE

When I finally arrived, it was dark. It had started to rain, and my brown hair clung to the sides of my face. The torches on the guard wall were ablaze, and I could see someone on duty, though it was impossible to tell who it was. I walked up to the gate, waiting for someone to notice me.

"Who the… Lucas?" I heard Jake call. I could hear the doubt in his voice, and it made me laugh. He must have thought I was dead. I felt like it sometimes, so he wouldn't be completely wrong.

"Yeah! Now can I come in?" I answered. After a few minutes the gate opened to reveal three smiling people. Noelle raced to give me a hug and Jake gave me a high-five. Kalos nodded in my direction but kept at a distance.

Jake was wearing a brown vest over a gray shirt and ripped jeans. He had clearly rushed to brush out

13

his black hair, and his green eyes were tired. He had a simple ring on one of his hands, just like any follower of a god.

Noelle, on the other hand, was wearing a green and black shirt with long sleeves, a pair of blue jeans, and a purple gem on a leather cord around her neck. Her long brown hair was pulled back into a braid. Her hazel eyes were bright and happy. She too had a ring on her hand.

"We're so glad you're back! What took you so long?" Jake asked.

I sighed. I wanted to just leave it with an *I don't want to talk about it,* but I knew that wouldn't work with them.

"It's a long, long story." He nodded, as if he understood. No, he definitely did not understand what had happened.

Noelle finally stepped back from me, her shirt wet from my drenched clothes. "Well, you're back, so we should probably have a quick meeting," she suggested.

We agreed and started walking towards the meeting room. Suddenly I remembered something.

"Wait. Where's Issrropia? Shouldn't she join us?"

The rest of the group stopped. Jake and Noelle glanced at each other nervously, and Kalos sighed.

"She ran into her temple a while ago. She wouldn't tell anyone why. We didn't want to bother her either. Just before you got here, she went to the dorms, probably to her room. If you want, you could go find her." I nodded and walked away towards the dorm room she was staying in, but first I had to stop at mine.

When I walked in the first thing I did was collapse onto my bed. I lay there a few minutes, deep in thought. Then I got up and put my shimmering gear away. I changed into dry clothes.

Before I continued towards Issrropia's room, I stopped to run my fingers over the familiar name tag on my door. It was a dark blue color, with dark green letters spelling my name.

Lucas. In the chaos I had almost forgotten my own name. It had been a long time since I had actually stayed here. I sighed and went to find Issrropia.

Kalos
God of Good

- Name means Well
- Carries an iron staff
- Represented by iron and emerald
- Wears a crown made of golden leaves
- two followers

6

MEETINGS

I walked down the hall until I spotted the gold and aqua name tag marking her room. I walked up and knocked. When she opened the door, her worry-filled frown turned into a smile of relief.

"LUCAS! Oh, I'm so glad you're okay!" She hugged me, taking me by surprise. When she finally let go, I told her that a meeting had been called and everyone needed to be present.

We walked together down the hall in silence. When we arrived at the meeting hall, she took me by the shoulders and looked me in the eyes. Her face was serious yet gentle.

"I just want you to know that I am extremely relieved you are okay. I was so worried about you." She gave me another quick hug, then put out her hand, making the doors open without even touching them, and we walked in.

Jake and Noelle were having an argument, Kalos

watching with an amused smile. He nodded at us, then cleared his throat. The two lovers instantly whipped around to face us, their faces red. They mumbled an apology as we took our seats. The five of us waited in uncomfortable silence until someone got the courage to speak.

"So...what did you find out, Lucas?" asked Jake awkwardly.

I thought back to what I had heard Max talking about. I didn't want to lie *or* die, so I told them what I had heard, not telling them I had been caught.

"So what took you so long?"

I flinched, then thought about what I should say. I knew I would have to lie, but what should I say? I had been hoping no one would question it, but being I had left early in the morning, I guess it was awfully suspicious. "I...got lost."

They slowly nodded and, with nothing else to talk about, the meeting was adjourned. It had been a long day, so I went straight to my room and instantly fell asleep.

I woke up the next morning to a knock at my door. Sitting up, I looked at the clock on the stand next to my bed: 9:43. So I had overslept. Maybe that was because I had barely got any sleep in the last few nights, maybe not.

"Lucas! We're having another meeting to make plans! Get up!" called Jake from the hall. I groaned quietly, but I stood up and got dressed. Then I met the rest of the group in the meeting hall. I stopped to grab some breakfast and sat down at the table.

I finally got a good look at Kalos. He was wearing Greek-style clothes; a white robe, brown sandals, a golden wreath. With his white beard and steady blue eyes, he reminded me of Zeus from the book of myths in the library.

Issrropia and Noelle looked like they were about to fall asleep, but Kalos and Jake were quite the opposite. They were awake and exited. I knew they both liked to make plans, so it wasn't really a surprise they were so energetic. After a few minutes of random chatter, we got to planning.

"So, using Lucas's information, we need to figure out where, when, how, and a plan B," said Kalos way too excitedly. I glanced around to the others, who, like me, were biting their lips to hold in their giggles.

"W-way to get to the point, Kalos!" Jake said, causing the table to erupt with laughter, leaving one very confused Kalos.

He tilted his head to the side and frowned. "What? What did I say?" None of us could answer, his confusion making us laugh even harder. When we finally got control of ourselves, we started to plan for real.

7

HELPING OUT

A few weeks later I was walking around the stables, petting the horses, mixing feed, and overall just trying to stay awake. The last few nights had been restless, the hours I had been able to sleep fewer and fewer. Nightmares had been keeping me awake constantly. It was always the same one; my friends turned against me, and I always ended up dead in the end. I had been running from base to base late at night, spying for both sides.

I looked over to my right to see Jake walking over to me. He stopped to pat his horse, which was right next to mine. After a few minutes he turned to me, a concerned look on his face.

"You've been tired a lot lately. Are you okay?"

I smiled and nodded, assuring him everything was fine. It wasn't, but he already had enough to worry about, so he didn't need me adding on to that list. He sighed.

"Just remember we are all here for you. If I'm pushing you too hard just tell me." There were a few more minutes of silence. Then he turned back to me, a smile on his face this time.

"Nice sword. Got a name for it?" It wasn't uncommon to have a name for your most powerful weapon, or your favorite one, or both. I thought for a minute, then smiled.

"How about *Vikin*? It's Greek for *victory*," I asked, letting out a chuckle.

Jake laughed too, then agreed with me. "*Vikin* it is then!" he said. And with that we continued a normal day for the first time in what felt like forever.

For the next few days, I continued to help out around the base. I worked in the gardens, improved the security system, and helped train Noelle in close combat. Everyone knew it, but no one wanted to admit it: war was coming.

By the time I was done with the security, everyone else was staring at me in shock.

"What?" I asked, confused with their fascination. Now they were facing the system in front of them.

"B-but how? Lucas, this is amazing!" cried Noelle.

I looked at the series of wires, levers, buttons, and metal I had created. All that was left was camouflaging it. I looked at the setting sun, deciding the work could wait until tomorrow. I grabbed my toolbox and started walking back to my room, but was stopped by Kalos and Jake.

Kalos' Base

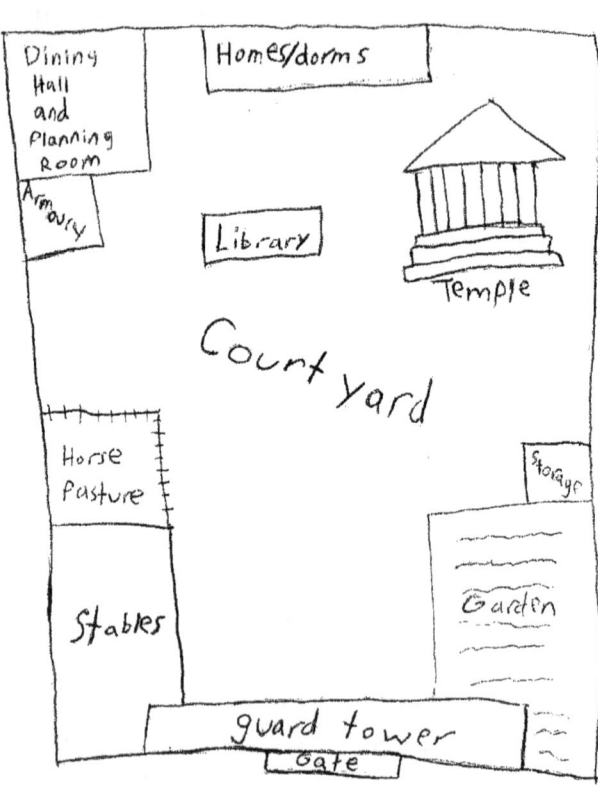

Dining Hall and Planning Room

Homes/dorms

Armoury

Library

Temple

Courtyard

Horse Pasture

Storage

Stables

Garden

guard tower

Gate

8

NEW MISSION

"Hey, Lucas. Look, we know you've been working hard all day, but we have a mission for you," said Jake, though he didn't seem as willing as he usually was.

I sighed. So much for getting some rest. "Explain."

This time it was Kalos' turn to speak. He sounded much more confident than Jake, but that made sense because he was a god. "We are planning to attack soon. We need you to get information to make sure that Katastrofi is not planning something that could jeopardize our plans. Will you do this for us one last time?"

I knew full well that this would not be my last time, but I finally agreed. I grabbed my supply bag and walked into the woods.

When I arrived at Max's base, I looked around to make sure no one else was there, then opened the door and quickly stepped in.

"Lucas?" called Max's voice from a few rooms away. I called back, letting him know it was me, and a few minutes later he came walking down the hall to greet me. "Wasn't expecting you here tonight. Do you have any information?"

I thought for a minute, then shrugged. A sort of friendship had formed between the two of us, or at least we were at peace.

"Jake and Kalos wanted me to come 'spy' on you. But I guess I do have some useful info."

Max sighed. I noticed that he wasn't quite as awake and aware as he usually was. I thought for a few more seconds, then said, "The defense system has been greatly upgraded. There are a ton of new traps—"

Max cut me off before I could continue.

"How many? Traps, I mean."

I paused. I had created so many, they were hard to count, but I told him an estimate, and he nodded. When I told him they were all manual, not automatic, and that he might be able to slip in while guards were switching, he seemed to perk up a tiny bit.

"You can go now, if you want." He thanked me for my help. I started to walk out, but I felt Max place a hand on my shoulder. "Wait."

I turned to face him, getting a good look at him for the first time that day. His black hair was unusually messy, and his dark eyes looked exhausted, as if he hadn't slept in a while. Then I realized that I must not have looked any better. Max frowned. When he finally spoke, his voice did not have the confidence and concentration it normally did.

"When war breaks out—and trust me, it will— just remember the generosity Katastrofi showed you, sparing your life." I froze, then turned and ran out the door.

My heart was beating wildly. As I walked away I remembered there was a clearing in the woods, so instead of going back to report to Kalos, I went there.

When I got there I found a rock near a pond and sat down. I put my head in my hands and took deep, shaky breaths. What had I done? Through all of the worries swirling around in my head, I realized I needed to make a plan of my own.

"I...should keep spying for Katastrofi...and Kalos... but—"

I was interrupted by someone jumping out of a tree. My head snapped up to see a furious Jake tackle me to the ground.

9

SECRETS REVEALED

"TRAITOR!" he screamed, anger burning bright in his eyes. I was shaking, scared, and alone.

"Jake, I—" I tried explaining what had happened, but Jake wasn't going to listen, and he wasn't going to let me talk.

"SHUT UP! HOW COULD YOU LIE TO US, LUCAS? How could you do this to us?" His screaming broke into a cracked whisper full of sadness and disbelief. The rage burning in him seemed to slow, but was not gone. I opened my mouth to reply but was cut off again.

"Careful with that temper of yours, Jake," said a familiar cold voice. Jake and I both turned our heads to see Max walk out of the woods, sword drawn and at the ready.

"What are you doing out here?" Jake answered this question by standing up and drawing his own sword. He kept me on my back by placing his heel on my chest.

"I could ask you the same thing, Max."

Max gave a wary smile, clearly confusing Jake. What was even going on anymore?

"I want to give this little traitor a piece of my mind. But now I see I'm not the only one who noticed he was acting strange." There was silence, the two opponents staring at each other, seeing who would make the first move.

Finally, Jake growled and yanked me to my feet, then turned back to Max. "As much as it pains me to say, we now have a common enemy for the moment. You can join us while we interrogate this traitor."

Common enemy? Me? How was this happening? "Please. Please stop," I whispered, my voice cracked with fear and sadness. I stopped and fell to my knees, suddenly dizzy. *They don't get it. They don't understand.*

"Get up," Max hissed. I felt his boot connect with the small of my back, sending a jolt of pain through my body. I was again pulled to my feet and forced to walk.

We didn't stop until we reached Kalos' base. Noelle met us at the gate. When she saw what was happening, a look of utter shock and hurt appeared on her face.

"What happened?" she cried. I had my hands crossed behind my back and my head was down. Jake slowed to a halt long enough to answer her.

"Go find Kalos and Issrropia. Emergency meeting."

She stared in disbelief at Jake as he pushed me again, shot a look of distrust and doubt at Max, and then ran off.

"Oh, wait! Noelle, come back!" Jake called. When she returned Jake whispered something in her ear. She looked confused for a second, then paled, but she nodded and sprinted away.

Jake forced me to walk again and next thing I know I'm alone in a jail cell. Max glared at me one more time as Jake locked the door; then the two of them walked out, leaving me to only my thoughts.

10

THE RINGS

The hot tears that I had been holding back for so long finally ran in rivers down my cheeks, and I didn't try to stop them. I fiddled with the ring on my finger, the ring showing I was a follower of Issrropia. I wanted to throw it off, but once on someone's finger, only the god the ring belonged to could take it off, and when they did it was not good. It meant you had betrayed them. *I'm sorry, Issrropia. I'm so sorry.*

My ring was gold, with a blue gemstone in the center. Engraved on the gem was a balance scale, the Scales of Balanced Power. Jake and Noelle's were silver and green, Max's red and black. I twisted the ring in circles, wondering what would happen next.

I didn't get any food that night. There were no windows, so time was impossible to tell without a watch, which I did not have. I assumed that it had only been a few hours, but with my hope and sanity slipping, it could have been days, or even weeks.

I could feel the insanity that clouded my thoughts; it was winning its battle against my sanity. I was a caged animal, just waiting for a chance to break free.

Sometime later, when I had my head in my knees and sobs racking my body, I heard the door opening. I glanced up to see Jake, Noelle, Kalos, and Issrropia walk in.

I looked back down, not wanting to look at anyone. I knew this was all my fault. I listened as the lock on my cell clinked open and someone stepped in, the door coming to a close behind them. Jake said something to them, but I didn't bother to listen to what it was.

I felt a gentle hand touch my shoulder. When I looked up it was Issrropia. She gave me a sad look, then turned to glare at the others and point towards the door back outside. They looked down but eventually left.

"Lucas, I'm so sorry!" she whispered, looking down, a tear rolling down her cheek.

I couldn't look her in the eyes. She looked a little bit sick, the unbalanced power and incoming war affecting her in an extremely negative way. Then she delivered the bad news I knew was coming.

"I have to take the ring. I'm so sorry. I'm doing what I can to prove you are innocent, but the boys won't listen. Noelle is helping you too." I felt sobs rack over me again, tears streaming down my face.

"Lucas," she said, her voice barely loud enough to hear, "give me your hand." After a few minutes, I finally raised my shaky hand. Issrropia place her hand under mine, keeping it steady, then pressed her finger to the gem on the ring, chanting under her breath. The ring flew off my finger and into her waiting palm.

I felt a sudden stabbing pain in my gut. I shouted and rolled over onto my side, clutching my stomach, knees to my chest, tears rolling nonstop down my face. As I lay there, whimpering and sobbing in pain, I heard Issrropia whisper, *"I'm so sorry, Lucas! I'm so, so sorry!"* Then she vanished in a dim flash of gold and blue, leaving me alone again.

After a few minutes the pain stopped, quickly replaced by a searing headache. I didn't move from the corner or the position I was in. I remembered my nightmares. Were they truly just dreams or were they more? If they weren't wrong... I shuddered, not wanting to think about it, and what might happen next.

The next few days were crazy. Every now and then someone, either Kalos, Issrropia, Jake, Noelle, or Max, would come into my cell, asking me an endless number of questions. I answered them with the truth every time, but they didn't listen. They didn't believe me.

11

NIGHTMARES TURNED REAL

T hen one day, about a week later, all of the others came in at once. I knew no one was likely to hurt me, so I allowed Jake to get a little bit closer. He sighed, and when he spoke he didn't sound angry, for the first time since this chaos started. He sounded tired.

"Your story matches ours, except for one big thing: you claim Katastrofi gave you the options, but he hasn't been seen for years, since the last war, *over one hundred years ago.* How is that possible?"

I stared at him, confused. Then it hit me: Max had lied. I pointed a shaky finger at Max. "Him. He is a liar. He summoned him, and he saw him. Tell the truth, please, Max."

Max glared at me and shook his head, but when Jake turned to him for an explanation, he put on a confused look. "I have no idea what he is talking about."

Jake growled, signaling his frustration. It went back and forth like this for a while, me calling Max a liar, Max claiming to be clueless. Jake grew more and more upset until finally, reaching his breaking point, he gave a shout. There was a bright flash, and a dagger appeared in his hand. "EVERYONE SHUT UP!" he shouted.

Max, now also upset, stormed out of sight. Jake turned to me. It was completely silent.

"Why won't anyone believe me? He's a liar," I pressed.

Jake started shaking. Issrropia had already walked out, unable to stand it any longer.

"Say one more word, any of you, and this dagger will be the last thing you see." Jake had gone crazy.

I was trembling in fear. Tears had started slowly falling down my cheeks. "Please. Please, someone rescue me from this mess," I whispered.

Jake whipped around and lunged at me. His dagger dug into my chest, opening a fatal wound. I screamed, and everything was silent. My breathing was ragged and painful, and I knew there was no way I would live.

The last thing I remember was Jake looking down at me, a mix of anger and shock on his face. The thing I noticed, though, was his eyes. Instead of the normal green they were supposed to be, they were a deep shade of red, almost like...no...almost like Katastrofi's.

I gasped, sending a sharp wave of fresh pain

through my body. Blood was pouring from the wound where the bloody knife was still buried deep into my body. The room was silent when darkness took over the world, and I knew I had breathed my last.

12

ISSRROPIA

I waked out of the room. This was getting out of hand. I should have told them the truth. I had seen everything. I ended up in my room. Sitting on my bed, staring at the floor, I realized this was mostly my fault. If I had told them immediately, would they have believed me? No, they would have told me I was crazy.

With my only follower accused of being a traitor, and everyone hating each other, I had been sick a lot. As the Keeper of Balance, the uneven balance in power had an effect on me.

My head jerked up when I heard shouting, then a scream. Not just any scream. Lucas's scream.

I space-jumped the cell to see a nightmare. Kalos and Noelle were trying to calm Jake, who was freaking out, going insane. But the worst part no one was looking at.

Lucas lay on the floor in a puddle of his own

blood, a dagger in his chest. His eyes were glassy, and his skin was white.

"NO! LUCAS! WHO DID THIS?" Noelle, who had given up on helping Kalos, raised a hand and pointed helplessly to Jake. I wanted to kill him right then and there, but then I felt pity for him.

I walked over to Lucas and carefully pulled the blade out. Then I picked him up and disappeared to my room.

I laid him on my bed, my blankets quickly soaked in his blood. I bandaged him up. I placed my hand in his and started chanting.

After a few minutes, Lucas shot up into a sitting position, gasping for air, eyes wild. He raised his shaky hands up to his face, and a look of disbelief and confusion passed over his features. Then he passed out.

I sighed. He would need a lot of rest, but he would get better. At least physically. If I had been a mortal and gone through what he had, I would have never recovered. That was what really worried me.

I made sure he was comfortable, checked that all of his wounds were bandaged, and sat down in the chair next to the bed. Within minutes I had fallen asleep, anxious of what I would witness when I woke up.

13

ALIVE

I woke up to find myself in a room full of blue and gold. Realizing I was in Issrropia's room, I started to panic. Then I was confused. Wasn't I supposed to be dead? What had happened?

I heard a relieved sigh from beside me. Turning, I saw Issrropia smiling. She rushed forward to give me a gentle hug, and then a rush of words tumbled out.

"Oh, I'm so glad you're okay! I thought you were gone for good! How are you feeling? Do you need anything? Is there something I can do for you?"

I gave a weak laugh. My chest felt like a fire was raging through it, but there was really nothing to do about it. "Other than feeling like complete trash, I'm fine. I could use something to eat though."

She grinned, and with a wave of her hand, a sandwich appeared in front of me. I devoured it and we talked for a bit. Then her smile dropped.

"I can't keep you hidden forever. What are we going to do about that?"

We thought for a few minutes. There was really no way around it. I would have to show I was alive at some point.

While I was thinking of an answer, I caught my reflection in a mirror in the corner of the room. I looked awful. My brown hair was messy, my dark eyes dull, my skin a little bit pale. I frowned.

"I guess it would be easier the sooner we do it. Not that I'm eager to, but..."

She nodded. We decided that tomorrow we would reveal me to the others, and if it didn't go well, she would protect me. I smiled.

"We've got a plan!" She told me to get some rest and I agreed with her instantly. I was out in minutes. Then the nightmares came.

I stood in a cell. Not mine, but another one in our base. In the center of the room stood Katastrofi and Jake. No one else was there. Katastrofi had his arms crossed and a glare on his face. His red eyes shone with hatred and power.

Jake looked as if he was being hypnotized, staring into space, or into the god's eyes. But behind the mask of oblivion, I could sense fear. Katastrofi shook his head.

"Why did I even try with you? You mortals are all worthless. Other than my loyal Max of course. I have no need for you anymore. Have fun explaining what happened to your friends!" Jake collapsed to the

ground, unconscious. Katastrofi laughed, then muttered to himself, "Two out of the way, only the girl to go. Then I can bother with my actual enemies!" With that he disappeared in a flash of black and red.

Jake groaned and sat up. He had a look of confusion on his face. He looked sick. Then I noticed the big thing: his eyes were back to normal! Katastrofi wasn't controlling him anymore, but what would the others think? Oh dear.

14

REVEALED

I sat up in a cold sweat. Shouts could be heard down the hall. Issrropia was pacing in front of the bed, but when I sat up she ran over to me and took my hand.

"You need to come with me, now. Something's happened."

I nodded, and a feeling of dread passed over me. I realized my dreams were visions, not just a wild mind. "I know. It's Jake, isn't it?"

She looked confused but nodded. Then she took my hand and within seconds we were in the jail.

We stood in front of Jake's cell, everyone in front of us. I leaned up against her to keep my balance. She cleared her throat. All of the other whipped around. Their faces went slack with shock, confusion, and disbelief.

"L-Lucas? Oh, Lucas!" Noelle ran up and hugged me. I smiled and hugged her back, then looked back over to the others. Max was shaking in anger, and a low growl escaped his throat. Everyone turned to him.

"You. You were supposed to die! This ruins everything!" He took a step toward me, but a steady voice rang out, making him stop.

"Not yet, Max. Not yet. Just wait."

Suddenly a black and red flash filled the room, and Katastrofi appeared in front of Max. Everyone froze.

"Someday you will regret everything you have done. Enjoy the peace while it lasts." With that he and Max disappeared from sight.

Everyone turned to me, then to Jake.

"I'm so sorry we ever doubted either of you!" cried Noelle. Then she fell to the floor in sobs. Walking out of his cell, Jake ran over to hug her. She jumped onto him, giving him a bear hug and a long kiss.

"Will you guys ever forgive us?" I smiled and looked at Jake, tilting my head as if asking his opinion. He laughed. "We forgive all of you!" we said, laughing.

And just like that everything was better. We shared stories about what had actually happened. Later that night, we had a celebration to honor the crazy events of the last few weeks. For the first time in a long time, everyone forgot about all their fears, and happiness was in the air.

The End?

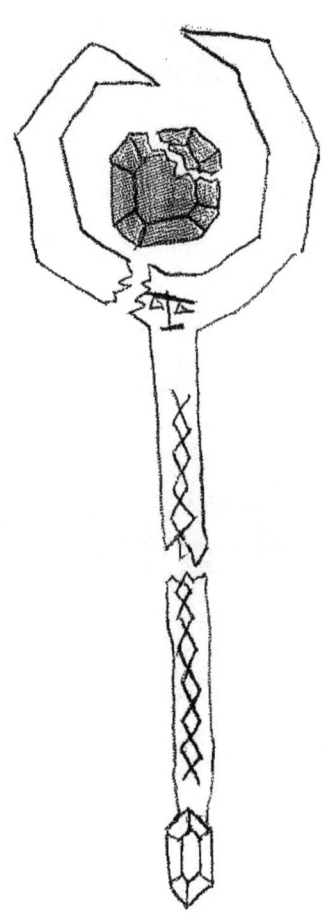

CPSIA information can be obtained
at www.ICGtesting.com
Printed in the USA
FFHW021707110619
52939178-58527FF